# VOYAGE
## TO THE
# PHAROS

by Sarah Gauch

*illustrated by* Roger Roth

Viking

The sun was just rising over the island of Rhodes as the giant ship with its great square sail and many oars pushed off. Dino clambered to the ship's deck and watched the people, houses, and shops—even the great statue of Helios, god of the sun—getting smaller.

Dino's father was the ship's cook, and for years Dino had pleaded to go with him on the long sea voyages to bring wine, oil, and leather to faraway places. Dino particularly wanted to see Alexandria, the Egyptian city founded by the mighty Greek leader Alexander the Great, with its shimmering palaces and giant temples. And the Pharos lighthouse. His papa said it was one of the tallest buildings in all the world, with statues of gods and great kings, a staircase that wound round inside—and at the very top a giant, roaring bonfire that guided ships from miles away to the city's shores. How he wanted to see it!

This time when he'd pleaded to go, his papa—whose hair had gotten grayer over the years and voyages—had finally said yes. And now here Dino was aboard the *Hermes* merchant ship, with a goose head on its stern, heading for the great city!

After the statue of Helios disappeared from the horizon, Dino set to work with his father, washing sacks of beans. He silently wished he could be on deck with the other men, hoisting and manning the sails, or even down below rowing with one of the twenty oars. But the crew was too busy to talk to him. No one even asked his name.

From the kitchen galley, Dino could feel the *Hermes* moving briskly across the water. It was spring, early to sail across the sea. In summer there were fewer treacherous gales, gales that could tear apart a fleet of one hundred ships. But the captain had insisted, and so far the weather was good, the wind strong.

"At this rate, we'll be in Alexandria in just four days," Papa said. "And then you'll finally see your Pharos lighthouse."

Dino reached up as high as he could. "A lighthouse so high it touches the sky," he said.

"If all goes well," Papa said.

That night Dino unrolled his blanket to sleep on deck with his father, staring at the stars that showed the way to Alexandria. Soon he fell asleep, imagining himself pulling the rigging and raising the sail. A brisk wind carried the *Hermes* along, and for a day the ship sped south.

Then, in the middle of the second night, Dino woke with a start. The wind was no longer brushing against his face, and he couldn't hear the heavy rush of water below. Instead all he heard was a lazy slapping of waves on the ship's hull. He stood up and saw the great square sail, limp and lifeless. The *Hermes* was barely moving at all.

"We'll never get to Alexandria at this pace," said a young, curly-haired man with a shrug. He was a bow sailor, Nicholas, who'd thanked Dino the night before for his bowl of beans.

"What can we do?" Dino asked nervously.

"Not much," the sailor said. "Just wait for the wind to start up again." He stared out to sea. "But better this than a spring storm."

Hours passed. Dino spent the day washing cabbage and chopping onions. He served the men their supper and then sat to eat with Papa. His stomach churned, not from the ship's rocking but from the stubborn silence.

Dino was getting ready to wash the dishes when he heard a familiar sound, the rustle of a sail, voices on deck.

He ran up the ladder. There was wind! Strong, glorious wind, brushing against his face and beginning to fill the great, square sail. He saw Nicholas and another sailor trying to untangle the rigging. When Dino jumped to help, Nicholas looked at him and smiled.

"Thanks, little monkey," he said.

Dino thought he'd burst—finally he'd done something besides make stew and wash dishes. And—finally—they were on their way to Alexandria. And the great lighthouse.

"If all goes well," Papa said, looking into the wind.

The next day was sunny, the wind strong and blustery. Dino had just begun cleaning some fish when he heard a frantic yell from above. On deck he ran right into a sailor.

"Brigands!" the man yelled, pointing out to sea.

Dino spun around. Sure enough, there was a ship with a black hull and square sail, just where the sky met the sea and, yes, it was headed right toward them!

Dino had heard many stories about sea brigands searching for big ships like the *Hermes*, full of wine and olive oil. Or, even more valuable, cargoes of Indian gems, ivory from Africa, or Phoenician cedar wood. In their small, swift ships the brigands would sidle up to the bigger merchant vessels and climb right on board.

The men on the *Hermes* worked feverishly, trying to capture the strongest gusts in the ship's sails. But the sails weren't enough. It was the rowers down below, who helped the *Hermes* get in and out of port—and escape trouble—who were working now, rowing as fast as they could, the sound of the oars like a hundred drums.

Dino ran to where the men were rowing, their arms moving back and forth, their backs shining with sweat in the hot, airless hull. As he watched, he got an idea. Dino darted to the galley, filled a clay pitcher with water, and ran back to the rowers. The first man grabbed the pitcher and guzzled, water falling from the sides of his mouth and onto his chest. Then Dino sprang to the next man and the next. It was as if they hadn't drunk for days.

Dino kept this up—sprinting from galley to rowers—until the yelling above had turned to a soothing murmur. He climbed to the deck. The black ship was still there, but smaller, and as Dino stared, it became smaller still. They had outrun the brigands!

The next day the sun rose over the Mediterranean, large and glowing. The air was cooler, the wind stronger, pushing the *Hermes* along faster than usual.

Nicholas said if all went well they'd see Alexandria the very next day. And the Pharos.

After serving the midday meal, Dino ran back to the deck and climbed a little way up the mast's rope ladder.

"What are you looking for, little monkey?" Nicholas called to him.

"The Pharos."

"Not yet," said Nicholas. "But soon."

Papa had walked up. "There are still the reefs and rocks."

Nicholas smiled up at Dino. "Don't worry, the Pharos will get us in."

That night on deck, Dino noticed that there were no stars in the sky. How would the *Hermes* get to Alexandria without stars to guide the way?

The next day the sky was gray and heavy. The waves were no longer soft and rolling but cresting like lions about to pounce. The ship was pitching up and down. Dino felt scared and alone.

Lurching from side to side, he went down to the galley to begin work. The captain and Nicholas were there, standing beside Papa, who looked different, worried.

"There's a storm coming," the captain shouted over the pounding waves. "I need every hand to hold the ship fast." He paused. "You like to help, boy. And you're light. I need a lookout to climb the mast—and I need him soon."

Dino's head reeled. Up the mast? In this storm? Papa put his arm around Dino.

"When you're up there," the captain continued, "watch for trouble . . . rocks, shallow reefs. And watch for a pinprick of light!" The Pharos.

"When?" Dino said.

"Soon," Nicholas replied.

As Dino worked in the galley the rest of the afternoon, the waves punching and pummeling the ship, he tried not to think of what lay ahead. He tried *not* to picture the *Hermes* being swallowed up by the raging sea.

Finally Nicholas beckoned him. On deck the wind was blowing in great gusts, making the sails shake and pull frantically, like birds flapping to get free. Waves crashed over the side, sending water rushing across the deck. Dino could see men wrestling with the sails, trying to tame them, to keep them cupped into the wind.

Nicholas held the ladder, and Dino began his slow climb up the mast, one wobbly rung at a time. The ladder, cold and slippery, swung and swayed with the battered ship. Dino's hands became raw as he climbed up through the rain and howling wind. His heart was beating so fast he thought he'd lose his balance.

At the top, Dino looked down at the black, angry sea below, the waves rising and crashing, the ship rocking like a toy boat in the surf. He took the rope that was tied around his waist and fastened it to the ladder to keep from falling. Then he looked toward the horizon for a pinprick of light. But he saw nothing, just a curtain of black night.

For what seemed like hours, he strained to keep his focus through the blustering rain. Then he saw it, hiding in the night's shadows, the light, like a star. It was the only one in the sky, in fact it touched the sky, just as his father had said. It was the lighthouse!

"The Pharos!" he yelled, pointing. "It's the Pharos!"

On the bow, Nicholas looked toward the light, then ran. "South by southwest! The Pharos!" he shouted to the bow sailors, who shouted to the stern sailors, who finally shouted to the steersmen. Together the crew struggled against the angry waves and gusting wind to turn the *Hermes*. Below deck, the rowers pulled at the clacking oars. And slowly, slowly, the ship's bow pointed toward the light.

Dino looked at the Pharos. Its fire was getting closer now, bigger. It made him feel stronger. As the *Hermes* sailed forward, the great lighthouse began to appear, not just the bonfire, but the first level, huge and sturdy. He imagined the spiral staircase inside that wound its way up and around, then the second level with its eight sides, and finally the third level with the great, blazing fire.

For an instant, Dino almost forgot the sheets of rain and his raw hands clinging to the rope. But then his body shivered from the wet and cold.

Hesitantly, he began climbing down. He took his glance from the Pharos to look at the sea below, the roaring waves rising then breaking into a fringe of white. Suddenly he saw in the swirl of white water ahead, shining in the Pharos's light, a big monster rock, black and jagged, hiding just beneath the waves.

"Shoal!" he yelled, pointing. "Shoal!" It couldn't have been more than ten boat-lengths away, and the *Hermes* was heading right toward it.

Nicholas saw it too. "To port!" he said, running toward the crew. "To port! Shoal!"

Again Nicholas's commands moved from the bow sailors to the stern sailors and finally to the steersmen. Dino kept his eye on the rock lit by the Pharos's great bonfire. Could they turn the ship?

Just as Dino felt the *Hermes* would surely hit the rock, the ship swayed and tilted, and slowly, very slowly, the bow began to turn toward the left. And slowly, very slowly, the *Hermes* passed the rock, its shiny, black fangs soon disappearing from sight.

Finally, Dino climbed down to the deck. When he looked up, there was the Pharos lighthouse looming ahead like a huge, friendly giant. Dino could see the building's dozens of windows now, the statues of the god Poseidon and of King Ptolemy.

And there, at the very top, was the giant bonfire. The Pharos not only touched the sky, it lit up the sky!

Gliding past the Pharos, the *Hermes* entered the harbor. They were safe.

Papa hugged Dino tight.

The winds had died down now, the rain nearly stopped. And the sun was just starting to rise over Alexandria like a giant gold coin.

From the deck, Dino could see the city's turreted walls, the palaces shining white in the morning sun, and the many-columned temple on the hill.

Amazing, thought Dino.

Nicholas patted Dino on the shoulder. "Well, little monkey," he said, "you got us in. Thanks be to Poseidon."

"Thanks be to the Pharos," Dino said. He looked back at the great lighthouse standing proud and tall, its fire still burning bright against Alexandria's dawn-lit skies.

# Author's Note

In its day, the nearly 400-foot Pharos lighthouse was an amazing structure that became the symbol of Alexandria. Even today no other lighthouse has been built as tall as the Pharos, one of the seven wonders of the ancient world.

Completed around 285 B.C., the lighthouse was a landmark at the mouth of Alexandria's harbor on an otherwise featureless coast. It is believed that after Alexander the Great's death in 323 B.C., his successor, Ptolemy I, decided to build the Pharos. He died before it was built, and his son and successor, Ptolemy II, oversaw the actual construction of the lighthouse.

The exceptionally sturdy Pharos lighthouse functioned for nearly 1700 years, until the earthquakes that continued to hit Alexandria's shores eventually left it in ruins. In 1477 A.D., Mamluk Sultan Qa'it Bay built his fort on the site of the lighthouse, even using some of its massive blocks, some believe. But where was the rest of the Pharos?

Some Alexandrians, historians, and archaeologists have maintained for years that the remains of the lighthouse lie in the sea right below the Qa'it Bay fort. An obvious conclusion. Still others have argued that the blocks, statues, columns, and capitals at the foot of the fort were just parts of ancient Alexandria's buildings, or pieces that the Ptolemites, Romans, and other Egyptian rulers brought from other parts of Egypt.

No one was really able to test these theories, since the Egyptian navy had closed these waters to the public for some fifty years, allowing few people to dive there. In 1994, however, a French archaeological team, headed by Jean-Yves Empereur, got permission to dive in the area and confirmed to their satisfaction that the stone blocks were from the Pharos lighthouse.

But just as it is a child, Dino, who helps bring the *Hermes* into Alexandria's great ancient harbor in this fictional story, it was the children of Alexandria who may have discovered the Pharos's remains first. For years—perhaps hundreds—Alexandria's boys and girls have swum the city's bays looking for and finding ancient artifacts from the civilization of the Ptolemites, the Romans, and others. It's possible that they discovered the great lighthouse under the sea before anyone else did. As with the other lingering questions still surrounding the Pharos, we can never be absolutely sure.

*To Rami and Samar, my adventurers.* —S.G.

With special thanks to archaeologist and scholar Jean-Yves Empereur, director of the Centre d'Études Alexandrines, whose extensive work excavating and studying the Pharos lighthouse has greatly expanded our knowledge of this magnificent building.

*In memory of my dad, Bernhard A. Roth, who shared his love of adventure with us.* —R.R.

VIKING
Published by Penguin Group
Penguin Young Readers Group, 345 Hudson Street, New York, New York 10014, U.S.A.
Penguin Group (Canada), 90 Eglinton Avenue East, Suite 700, Toronto, Ontario, Canada M4P 2Y3
(a division of Pearson Penguin Canada Inc.)

Penguin Books Ltd, Registered Offices: 80 Strand, London WC2R 0RL, England

First published in 2009 by Viking, a division of Penguin Young Readers Group

1  3  5  7  9  10  8  6  4  2

LIBRARY OF CONGRESS CATALOGING-IN-PUBLICATION DATA IS AVAILABLE
ISBN: 978-0-670-06254-6

Manufactured in China     Set in Centaur MT